nickelodeon

RISE OF THE TEENAGE MUTANT NINJA TURTLES

WHEN MUTANTS ATTACK!

adapted by David Lewman

illustrated by Patrick Spaziante

based on the teleplay "The Evil League of Mutants"
by Jesse Gordon

Random House 🏠 New York

Raph thinks he and his three
brothers need more training.
He asks their father, Splinter,
to help them.

Dear Parents:

Congratulations! Your child is taking the first steps on an exciting journey. The destination? Independent reading!

STEP INTO READING® will help your child get there. The program offers five steps to reading success. Each step includes fun stories and colorful art or photographs. In addition to original fiction and books with favorite characters, there are Step into Reading Non-Fiction Readers, Phonics Readers and Boxed Sets, Sticker Readers, and Comic Readers—a complete literacy program with something to interest every child.

Learning to Read, Step by Step!

Ready to Read   Preschool–Kindergarten
• big type and easy words • rhyme and rhythm • picture clues
For children who know the alphabet and are eager to begin reading.

Reading with Help   Preschool–Grade 1
• basic vocabulary • short sentences • simple stories
For children who recognize familiar words and sound out new words with help.

Reading on Your Own   Grades 1–3
• engaging characters • easy-to-follow plots • popular topics
For children who are ready to read on their own.

Reading Paragraphs   Grades 2–3
• challenging vocabulary • short paragraphs • exciting stories
For newly independent readers who read simple sentences with confidence.

Ready for Chapters   Grades 2–4
• chapters • longer paragraphs • full-color art
For children who want to take the plunge into chapter books but still like colorful pictures.

STEP INTO READING® is designed to give every child a successful reading experience. The grade levels are only guides; children will progress through the steps at their own speed, developing confidence in their reading.

Remember, a lifetime love of reading starts with a single step!

Step into Reading, Random House, and the Random House colophon are registered trademarks of
Penguin Random House LLC.

Visit us on the Web!
StepIntoReading.com
rhcbooks.com

Educators and librarians, for a variety of teaching tools, visit us at RHTeachersLibrarians.com

ISBN 978-0-593-11909-9 (trade) — ISBN 978-0-593-11910-5 (lib. bdg.)

Printed in the United States of America   10 9 8 7 6 5 4 3 2 1

Splinter tells the Turtles
to study the fights
in old movies.
The Turtles have already
seen these movies.
They do not think
this is good training!

The hero in the movies uses
fish and ladders as weapons!
The Turtles say they will *never*
fight with fish and ladders.

Splinter gets *mad*!
He tells the Turtles
they are grounded!
He also takes away
their weapons.

Baron Draxum is an evil villain.

He is a scientist.

He uses vines as weapons.

Years ago, he created

the Teenage Mutant Ninja Turtles!

Now he wants the Turtles
to join him.
If they refuse, Baron Draxum
will destroy them!

Baron Draxum has two henchmen,
Muninn and Huginn.
They are gargoyles.
But he needs more help
to beat the Turtles, so he
sends for more evil mutants!

Hypno-Potamus used
to be a magician.
Now he's a mutant hippo!
He can hypnotize people.
He can throw
sharp rings at the Turtles.

The Sando Brothers used
to be circus acrobats.
Now Carl and Ben are
mutant crabs!
They can shoot claws
at the Turtles.

Repo Mantis is a
giant mutant praying mantis.
He is strong and mean.
His pincers are like sharp
metal hooks.

Meat Sweats used
to be a TV chef
named Rupert Swaggart.
Now he is a mutant pig!
He can smack the Turtles
with his big hammer.

Warren Stone used to be
a TV news anchor.
Now he is a mutant worm!
He wears an armored glove
he stole from a museum.
It can blast energy!

Together, they are Baron Draxum's
Evil League of Mutants!
They want to defeat the Turtles!

Baron Draxum has a plan to corner the Turtles so his Evil League can fight them.

The Turtles sneak out of the lair.
Ads for a show with free pizza
blow into their faces.
The star of the show is
a robot-dinosaur magician!
The Turtles decide to go.

But when the Turtles
get to the show,
all they find is
an empty warehouse.
It is dark and scary inside.

Baron Draxum steps out
of the darkness.
The Turtles are surprised.
He asks the Turtles
to join him.
They refuse.

Baron Draxum tells
his mutants to attack!
They blast the Turtles
through the wall
and into the next building!

The Turtles land.

They groan and moan.

But when they look around,

they see lots of fish and ladders—

just like in Splinter's movies!

They can use Splinter's training to fight Baron Draxum's mutants!

Meat Sweats swings his
big hammer at Raph.
Raph blocks the hammer
with a ladder!

Mikey steps on Warren Stone.
He uses a ladder to knock
Repo Mantis away!

Hypno-Potamus throws his
sharp rings at Donnie.
Donnie dodges the rings.
Then he throws a ladder
right at Hypno-Potamus!

The mutant crabs
shoot claws at Leo.
He bats the claws away
with a swordfish.
Then he smacks
the brothers with the fish!

The Turtles win the fight!
They beat Baron Draxum's
Evil League of Mutants
with fish and ladders!

Splinter's training

really works!

Back in their lair, the Turtles
tell Splinter they are sorry.
He was right.
They *can* win a fight
with fish and ladders!

Splinter apologizes
for getting so mad
at his sons.